J PC
PIC
MON

Monk, Isabell.

Blackberry stew.

BLACKBERRY STEW

BLACKBERRY STEW

by Isabell Monk
illustrated by Janice Lee Porter

Carolrhoda Books, Inc./Minneapolis

Grandpa Jack had passed away. Aunt Poogee and I sat on her wraparound porch, all dressed up. We watched as our family and friends arrived at the church up on the hill for his funeral.

All of my family were there—
Grandpa Vince, Grandma Kate,
Uncle Tuney, Aunt Frances, my
cousins and, of course, Grandma
Jane and my mom and dad. They
brought special family treats and
lots of hugs and kisses. I kept
thinking how much Grandpa Jack
would have loved seeing my whole
family get together.

"Hope, it's time to go up the hill, honey," my
mom said. I couldn't answer because there was a
lump in my throat the size of a walnut.

Aunt Poogee answered for me, "Eve, I'll bring
her just as soon as I finish up the blackberry stew."

My mom nodded and headed up the hill.

After she left, I looked up at Aunt Poogee.

"My goodness, your big brown eyes are just spilling over with tears. Even filled with tears, they are the spitting image of your grandpa Jack's," she said as she handed me one of her lacy hankies.

Aunt Poogee looked sad too. Grandpa Jack was her big brother.

"I'm afraid to go to the funeral," I said.
"Once we say good-bye to Grandpa Jack, I'll
never see him again."

"Never see him again?" Aunt Poogee
repeated. "You really think so?"

She closed her eyes, cocked her head to
the side, and said, "I can see him right now
with my eyes shut. I can see him
sitting in that chair, rocking you
to sleep when you were a baby."

I closed my eyes and cocked my head too, but I couldn't see him.

"Oh my," Aunt Poogee cooed, "I can see us fishing on the river for hours, catching nothing but a cold. Can't you just imagine him in those overalls of his?"

Grandpa Jack loved wearing his funny old overalls with the holes in the back.

"Remember that day last summer?" Aunt Poogee said. "The day after you came to stay with me . . . while your grandpa Jack was visiting?"

"When we went blackberry picking?" I asked.

Aunt Poogee nodded.

"We really got a surprise that day!" I said.

"We certainly did," she said, as the corners of her mouth turned up to make a smile. "Baby, I'm going in to finish up the blackberry stew, OK?"

As I remembered that day, I started to see Grandpa Jack.

"The blackberries are ripe and ready for picking," Grandpa Jack had said. I could see him in my mind's eye, like he was standing right in front of me.

Grandpa Jack had told me that I'd have to get up early. "We'll be up so early that we'll see the sun and the moon in the sky at the same time," he said.

"Grandpa," I asked, "what will we do once we pick all those blackberries?"

"We'll get to eat 'em," he chuckled. "Mmmm, you know I love me some *de-lic-ious* blackberry stew!"

Especially the stew his and Aunt Poogee's mama used to make. She was my great-grandma and had died long before I was born. *All* the older folks in our family still talk about Mama Nellie's blackberry stew.

The next morning, I jumped out of bed—
I was so excited to go blackberry picking.
Even though it was warm, I covered myself
with clothes from head to toe just like
Grandpa Jack told me to. I even made sure
my pants were stuck down into my socks
so nothing, no brambles or sticks or *bugs*,
could get in there.

Then we put on our blackberry-picking
gloves. They had no fingers! Grandpa Jack
had cut them off so we could pick the
berries without the thorny brambles pricking
our hands.

Finally, we were ready to pick
blackberries!

I ran over to those blackberry bushes. I couldn't wait to get started. Grandpa Jack chuckled behind me, "Poogee, when you and I were kids, we'd race to those bushes too!"

We picked for a long, long time. The sun came up, but we kept on picking. Sometimes I stopped to eat a berry right off the vine, hot from the sun. It melted in my mouth, seeds and all. We ate almost as many berries as we picked, and we filled buckets and buckets and buckets with sweet, juicy blackberries.

Just as we were filling the last bucket to the tippy-top, I saw something sliding along under the blackberry bushes. It was low and dark. I thought maybe it was a mole or a field mouse.

Aunt Poogee and I crept closer. A small slit of an eye winked at us and suddenly a long, pale green body darted toward us.

"Snake!" we screamed at the same instant.

"There's a snaaaaake!" I shrieked again and jumped back. What if it were a ferocious rattlesnake or even a cobra!

Grandpa Jack ran over. He picked up a really long stick, leaned over, and scooped up the snake.

"Look here!" he laughed. "This is just an old garter snake. This fellow wouldn't hurt anybody. He's our friend. He keeps the mice away from the house."

"How does he do that?" I asked, stepping a bit closer.

"He eatsssss 'em," hissed Grandpa Jack.

He swung the snake on the stick so that I could get a better look, but it nearly touched Aunt Poogee. She jumped back.

"Jack, you know I hate snakes," she huffed and hightailed it back to the house.

I looked at the snake. I took one step
forward and stopped.
"Are you still afraid of him?" Grandpa Jack
asked me. I nodded.
"He's afraid of you too. Here, give me your hand."
Grandpa Jack gently put my hand on the snake.
His strength and courage seemed to pass from his
hand to mine. "Don't be scared little snake,"
I said as I stroked its back.

The snake *looked* cold and slimy, but it wasn't.
It was dry and warm from the summer soil.
Grandpa Jack put the snake back on the path,
and it slithered into the woods.
"Yeah, go on that way, little
buddy," he said.

Grandpa Jack and I walked back to the house with the overflowing buckets. He showed me how to rinse the berries in a big aluminum tub in the backyard and how to pick out the extra leaves and twigs.

That night, Aunt Poogee made Mama Nellie's blackberry stew. The stew was so warm and gooey-good, just like I felt when I was with my grandpa Jack.

"There's nothing better than picking blackberries and eating blackberry stew," said Grandpa Jack.

"Well, maybe meeting a sssssssnake!" I added.

I can still hear Grandpa Jack laughing
at that. Even Aunt Poogee had chuckled.

Up on the hill, the church bell rang.
"Hope?" Aunt Poogee asked as she took
off her apron. "Are you ready to go?"

"I think I'm ready now," I answered. "I can see Grandpa Jack in my mind's eye, just like you said."

"Your grandpa Jack lives on in our memories, Hope," Aunt Poogee told me. "He lives on in you too."

"Grandpa Jack will be with us whenever we tell stories about him," I said. "And he'll be with us whenever we eat blackberry stew."

I took Aunt Poogee's hand.
I felt braver now, like I had when
I touched the garter snake.
Grandpa Jack had shown
me that I could be brave.

Together, Aunt Poogee and I walked up the hill to join our family. It was time to say good-bye to Grandpa Jack—but, I reminded myself, only until we share the next story or some blackberry stew.

MAMA NELLIE'S BLACKBERRY STEW*

Crust:
2 cups all-purpose flour
4 teaspoons baking powder
1 teaspoon salt

¼ cup sugar
2 tablespoons butter or shortening
1 cup milk

Mix and sift the dry ingredients. Work in the shortening with your fingers, two knives, or a pastry cutter. Gradually add milk to make a soft dough. Set aside.

Filling:
3 cups fresh blackberries, rinsed,
   or 1 package (24 ounces) frozen
   blackberries, thawed
1 cup sugar
2 tablespoons all-purpose flour

⅛ teaspoon salt
3 tablespoons lemon juice
1 tablespoon butter, plus
   enough butter to grease
   the pan

Preheat oven to 450°F.
In a large bowl, mix sugar, flour, salt, and lemon juice. Add berries and stir to coat with mixture.
Place berry mixture in a greased (with butter) deep-dish pie pan or a casserole dish. Cut one tablespoon of butter into small pieces and scatter over mixture.
Spoon large drops of crust mixture over the top of the berry mixture.
Bake 10 minutes at 450°F.
Lower heat to 350°F and bake for 20–30 minutes.
Remove from oven. Cool slightly and serve.
A scoop of vanilla ice cream makes it a real treat.
Enjoy!

*Ask an adult to help.

This book is dedicated to the memories of Mr. Samuel Judge,
Mr. Richard Yoakam, and Mr. Martin Thomas,
three beloved grandpas.
Thanks to Sara Saetre, Ellen Stein, and Patrick J.
O'Connor for their help and support — I.M.

This one's for Joe — J.L.P.

Text copyright © 2005 by Isabell Monk
Illustrations copyright © 2005 Janice Lee Porter

Carolrhoda Books, Inc.
A division of Lerner Publishing Group
241 First Avenue North
Minneapolis, MN 55401 U.S.A.

Website address: www.carolrhodabooks.com

Library of Congress Cataloging-in-Publication Data

Monk, Isabell.
    Blackberry stew / by Isabell Monk ; illustrated by Janice Lee Porter.
       p.   cm.
    Summary: When her Grandpa Jack dies, Hope remembers the time she went
  with him to pick blackberries, and she realizes that he will continue to live in
  her and in her memories.
    ISBN: 1–57505–605–4 (lib. bdg. : alk. paper)
    [1. Death—Fiction. 2. Grandfathers—Fiction. 3. Memory—Fiction.
  4. Blackberries—Fiction.] I. Porter, Janice Lee, ill. II. Title.
  PZ7.M75115Bla 2005
  [E]—dc22   2004002562

Manufactured in the United States of America
1 2 3 4 5 6 – JR – 10 09 08 07 06 05